Jubilant Jeremy Johnson

by Doreen Harrison

WIPF & STOCK · Eugene, Oregon

Wipf and Stock Publishers
199 W 8th Ave, Suite 3
Eugene, OR 97401

Jubilant Jeremy Johnson
By Harrison, Doreen
Copyright©2015 Apostolos
ISBN 13: 978-1-5326-6938-5
Publication date 9/23/2018
Previously published by Apostolos, 2015

Dedicated to all the children in my life

Contents

The School Concert

John Jeremy Johnson was a young boy who belonged to a very talented musical family. His mother was an opera singer who sang with famous choirs and performed at sell-out solo converts. Jeremy's mum was occasionally joined on stage by his father, who was himself an accomplished singer with a magnificent tenor voice. The couple had appeared together on various television programmes in several countries and performed in operas and concerts all over the world. Jeremy had two sisters: Joanne was fourteen and Juliet was twelve. Joanne was a pretty good musician and had already passed her eighth grade in piano, which meant that she could sometimes play the music for her parents, especially at the smaller charity concerts. She also played the flute, oboe and clarinet, passing all her music exams with distinction. Juliet played the violin, viola and cello. She was so talented was she that had already performed violin solos in her parents' gala concerts in London, Rome and Prague; making a name for herself as a child prodigy: a wonder musician.

Ten-year-old Jeremy, on the other hand, had no particular musical ability. They had christened him John Jeremy after his father; but the name appeared to be the only thing the two had in common. As he grew up, Jeremy had been introduced to all kinds of musical instruments, and given music lessons, but all to no avail. Jeremy was a non-starter as far as music was concerned – he was tone deaf! As a member of the Johnson family, you can be sure that his lack of musical talent was a great disappointment to his parents and a real embarrassment for Jeremy.

Because the family were in great demand for operas and concert appearances across Europe, Mrs Johnson had decided to home school her children. So, for much of the year, they lived and travelled in a bright red mobile home, which was neither more nor less than a converted double-decker bus.

On the ground floor of this remarkable rolling residence was a well equipped kitchen, a small school room and a larger area for eating, playing and watching television. During the day this room also served as the practice room for their concerts; whilst in the night the seats were folded down into a bed for Mr and Mrs Johnson. On the upper deck there was a bathroom and two small bedrooms, each with bunk beds and a wardrobe. The bathroom always had hot water, since whenever Mr Johnson—the sensible man—parked the bus he always chose a well serviced site so that he could hook up to electricity and water.

Such a deluxe mobile home cost a lot of money, but the Johnsons were well able to afford it, being well paid for their professional skills. Mr Johnson was very proud of this unique vehicle and had the words, "Jubilant Johnsons" written in large letters across both sides. Whenever he was driving, Mr Johnson would encourage Jeremy by telling him that one day he would have the important job of driving the bus.

Every morning and evening, the family would meet together in the happy clutter of the downstairs room to pray and read from the family Bible. This was a special time for Jeremy; he loved the closeness of his family, even if he was the odd one out musically. He never really thought much about whether or not God heard or answered their prayers – it was just something they all did together because mum and dad were Christians.

One summer, the family had a series of concerts in the North of England and since they would be there for three months, Mrs Johnson decided to allow herself a holiday from teaching at home and send the children to local schools. Jeremy jumped with delight when he heard the news! At last, a chance to meet and play with other boys his own age; boys who couldn't sing a note; boys who couldn't care less about playing pianos or oboes; boys just like him!

In reality, school meant lessons and hard work, but Jeremy didn't care; all that mattered to him was the sport and rough and tumble way he played with the boys after school and at playtime. Every day he would arrive back at the bus dirty and dishevelled but well satisfied with the day's fun. It was the best summer he had ever had! Yet even as he played, Jeremy could not get away from the shadow of his family. His new friends were very curious to know what it was like to live as one of the famous Jubilant Johnsons and when they were allowed round to tea they were very impressed with the double decker mobile home.

Then it happened! There was to be a school concert at the end of term, and Mr Phelps the head teacher wanted all the pupils in the oldest class to take part. Some were already in the school choir, whilst others performed music in a small ensemble and the school gymnastics club had put together an amazing sequence of jumps and balances for the show. As the Headmaster ticked off the names of each pupil taking part in the concert, he looked up. "Ah, Jeremy," he said, "Your turn. Since you are one of the Jubilant Johnsons, a truly talented family, perhaps we could use your talents to open our concert – you can be our star performer! What would you like to do for us?"

Jeremy nearly choked; but he kept his wits about him. He quickly worked out that his parents' next performance was in London and so he would probably have left the school before the concert. All the same, here was an opportunity to have what he had always wanted: his name on a concert programme, just like dad. It would probably be the only chance he would ever get; and so never mind what he *should* have said, what actually Jeremy *did* say was, "Oh yes Sir! I'd be delighted to sing the opening solo!"

So the programmes were hastily printed, and on the front, in large letters, was the announcement, "Special Guest Soloist: John Jeremy Johnson."

Jeremy proudly took his copy of the programme to read on the way home; but as he came near the bus he hid it as best he could inside his coat. He simply couldn't show it to the family. Perhaps when they had moved on he would bring it out so that his mother could display it, like she did with other programmes of the family's concerts. However, Jeremy still felt rather worried about misleading his teacher and lying to his school friends; what would they think of him when they found out? No problem, he thought, I'll just pretend I didn't know we were going away, and that I'm sorry I can't sing at the concert after all.

Then it all went wrong. One evening, not long after Jeremy had brought the programme home, his dad had an important announcement to make over dinner. "Jeremy," he said, "I know how much you have enjoyed being at school this summer and I didn't want you to miss out on all the special end of term activities. So I've agreed with the opera company that we won't begin any concerts in London until after term ends. We'll be here for sports day, the school trip and the end of term concert."

Jeremy was horrified! What could he do? His mother was too shrewd to be fooled by any suggestions of stomach ache, headache or any other imaginary ache he might invent. So far he had managed to keep his friends in the dark by informing them that he could not take part in concert rehearsals, because he wanted his solo item to be a surprise on the night. "Blimey! It'll be a surprise alright!" thought Jeremy.

9

That night, Jeremy couldn't sleep. There were only two days left before the concert, and his name was on the front of the glossy programme. What could he do? Eventually, he gave in, and went to see his dad. Dad never went to sleep early; he was practicing scales on a portable keyboard with his headphones on in case he woke the children. Jeremy showed dad the programme for the school concert and humbly explained his predicament. Dad listened carefully to Jeremy; and when he had finished said, "We can't expect the school to reprint all the programmes. I think we had better pray to God and ask him what to do." So that is what they did. Jeremy's dad asked God for wisdom to know the right thing to do, and for his help in making everything work out for good. Jeremy felt quite relieved; he didn't know why but the concert didn't seem to matter so much as it had.

All the same, by the night of the concert, Jeremy began to feel really sick. He could see his mother and sisters sitting in the front row to watch Jeremy – the star performer – sing his solo. As Jeremy sat with his class mates on the platform, he wished the floor would open up and swallow him. The hall was packed; all the seats were full and a large crowd of people were standing at the back.

Soon Mt Phelps came to the front of the stage, wearing a smart blue suit for the occasion with a red carnation in his button hole. He thanked everyone for coming and then he announced, "Ladies and gentlemen, to open our school concert tonight I am proud to present to you the world famous tenor—Mr John Jeremy Johnson." Jeremy's jaw dropped; he thought he would die on the spot. He began to get up out of his chair to face the inevitable when he suddenly noticed that the cheering crowd were not looking at him at all; they were not even looking in his direction. As Jeremy followed their gaze he saw someone—a man—appearing from the other side of the stage. The man came and took the microphone from Mr Phelps, took a bow and began to sing. It was Jeremy's dad! What a relief! Jeremy nearly forgot to sit back down. So they were getting John Jeremy Johnson to sing at the school concert after all – only it was the father and not the son. When Jeremy's dad finished his performance the whole audience stood to clap and shouted, "Encore!" Mr Johnson raised a hand for quiet, and then announced, "I expect you were surprised to see me here, after all, this is the pupils' end of term concert. However, you have accepted my only son, Jeremy, into your school, and treated him well. This has been my way of saying thank you to everyone. And now - let the show go on."

That night, at family prayers, Jeremy was happy but unusually quiet. Dad got out the family Bible and read a verse:

"Once, Jesus Christ suffered for our sins, the righteous for those who were not righteous, in order to bring us to God" from 1 Peter 3:18.

"Stop dad!" Jeremy suddenly came awake. "I know what that verse means! You took my place tonight. You sang on stage to get me out of the mess I got myself into. That's what it means – God's son Jesus took my place and got me out of the mess I was in. He took the punishment I deserved for my sin by dying on a cross before coming alive again. It is because of him I can come near to God; and it's because of him that God hears my prayers."

And that night, for the first time that he could remember, Jeremy really meant it when he—not out loud but in his heart—said thank you to God for answering his prayers and for solving his problem.

The Stolen Violin

Jeremy's sister Juliet was already being acclaimed around the world as a child prodigy on account of her musical ability. Indeed, following one recent concert performance a distinguished, older violinist had presented her with a unique gift. "It is a Stradivarius violin," the old man explained, "I have played it for many years. But now since I have no family or grandchildren to leave it to, I give it to you in return for your beautiful playing tonight!" Mr and Mrs Johnson were amazed: the violin was worth many thousands of pounds! Mr Johnson offered to pay for it, but the old man declined. He had no need of money, but he wanted to know that his precious violin would be in the hands of a master artist like Juliet and used to make marvellous music.

So the violin travelled with them on the big double-decker bus, housed in an old battered case which was lined with red velvet. You could tell, just by looking at the case, that it had something important inside. Mr Johnson—realising the value of the violin—at once had it insured in case of loss, accidental damage or theft; and Juliet's already superb playing reached new levels of excellence by virtue of her handling using such an extraordinary instrument.

Everyone seems pleased for Juliet – everyone except Jeremy. He was so jealous of his sister! Whenever Juliet carried the violin in its case, people would stop and say flattering things about her. Some would even exclaim, "She must be an accomplished musician—look at that special case!" Jeremy scowled – he wanted to be someone important one day.

The family had arrived in a new area, and posters with pictures of Juliet playing her violin were everywhere. They carried the announcement, in large letters, of the time and place of Juliet's performances, and then, this sentence: *"Come and hear the music of this amazing instrument, played by the young, talented member of the Johnson family"*.

Jeremy had an alluring idea. Juliet's name wasn't on any of the posters, so if he just borrowed the violin and carried it around—just a little way, for just a little while—people would think he was the young and talented virtuoso.

The violin, in its case, was kept in a locked in Juliet's wardrobe. Jeremy fetched the key—he knew where all the keys were kept—and carefully opened to door. Gently, he took out the violin in its case and quietly re-locked the cupboard. Feeling somewhat like a thief, Jeremy took the priceless stolen goods back into his room. Removing the valuable violin from its case, he covered it with a black plastic bin liner and hid it down the side of his bed. Then, carrying only the empty case, he set off for the town.

Jeremy's plan was a complete success! With the Jubilant Johnson posters everywhere, it wasn't long before people began to call out, "Look, there's the Johnson's boy carrying a violin case! He must be the famous violin prodigy! Jeremy tried to look musical; he thought of whistling a famous tune, but he didn't know any. Someone actually took a photograph of him with the case. He enjoyed his walk of fame.

At last Jeremy could pretend that he was really one of the musically talented in the Jubilant Johnson family; and that felt good. After his walk, Jeremy made his way back to the bus, being very careful to keep the violin case out of sight. As he climbed up stairs to his own room, he was already planning his next visit to the town. Reaching across his bed, he felt for the plastic bin liner in which he had hidden the violin—it wasn't there! The black bag had gone! He pulled the covers off the bed

—he got down on his knees and looked under the bed —but there was no bin liner and no violin!

Jeremy rushed to the window. Throwing it open, he was about to shout, "Help! Thieves!" until he remembered that *he* was the thief. What could he do; where was the violin?

Across the yard near the entrance to the caravan site, Jeremy saw the town garbage-collection truck. His heart almost stopped —the workmen were tossing plastic bin liners into the truck, and Jeremy could hear the heavy grinding sound of rollers mashing up the bags and their contents into a smelly mush inside the machine. Jeremy had the sickening thought that a Stradivarius violin would shriek with pain at such treatment.

Jeremy turned from the window and rushed downstairs. He ran as fast as he could to the lorry and begged the men to stop. The men just stared back at Jeremy, wondering what all the fuss was about. By now, Jeremy's dad had caught up with him; he had seen him run yelling from the bus. Jeremy flung himself into his father's arms. "Dad, I took Juliet's violin and put it in a plastic bin liner. I carried the case into the town pretending to be a famous musician. Now the bin liner has gone. They've chucked it in the garbage truck!"

"It's OK," said his dad, apologising to the garbage collectors, and "just carry on, everything's alright." Dad took gently Jeremy by the hand back into the bus, and calmed him down. Then he opened one of the wardrobes and pulled out the violin. He explained. "I saw the bin liner down the side of your bed Jeremy, and I decided to check the contents before I put it with the rest of the garbage. Good job I did! Now I think you'd better put the violin back into its case and put them both back safely in Juliet's wardrobe." Tears were pouring down Jeremy's face.

"Oh, dad," he said, "what is to become of me? I'm a thief!" His dad put his arm around his son. "Jeremy," he said, "You took the violin because you wanted to be special. But God made you with the same love and care as he made Juliet and Joanne; it's just that you all have different gifts. Maybe not all of those gifts have come out yet, but hey will, you'll see. God was watching over you today and you can always depend on Him to care for you."

They could hear Juliet outside, saying rather importantly, "I am just going to fetch my violin so that I can practice for the concert." Dad took the case with the violin inside and went to the top of the stairs. "I've got it out ready for you, Juliet," he said and, with a reassuring smile towards Jeremy, he took it to her.

That night at family prayers, Jeremy was almost expecting his dad to read a chapter about a naughty boy who stole his sisters' violin so that he could be a show off. He didn't know if there was such a story in the Bible, but thought their probably was. Instead, dad read about God always forgiving people who admitted that they had done wrong. The verse was:

If we confess our sins, he is faithful and just to forgive us our sins, and to cleanse us from all unrighteousness" from 1 John 1:9.

Later, after prayers, when everyone else had gone to bed and he and dad were alone, Jeremy asked if he could pray and tell God he was sorry for what he had done. Jeremy prayed, "Dear God, I am sorry for stealing Juliet's violin, please forgive me." And having done so, he kissed his mum and dad, went up to bed, and slept soundly.

The Moving Music

Very often, the Jubilant Johnsons were kept busy with individual performances and solo concerts, but just occasionally they were able to perform together. Whenever they did so, they needed to use specially prepared written music, which included lines of notes for each of them to follow.

Since this music had been specially composed and arranged for them, it could not be bought in the shops. In fact, so far as Mr Johnson knew, there were only two copies in existence: one was kept by the composer, and the other was taken by the Johnsons on their tour. Mr Johnson kept this essential manuscript in a leather music case which had belonged to him since he was Jeremy's age. "The special music will always be in its special place," he said. "We don't want to mix it up with anything else!"

The Johnsons were billed to take part in a very grand charity concert at the Royal Albert Hall, London. The Prince of Wales was expected to attend, since he was a patron of that particular charity; and large billboard posters appeared all over London to promote the concert – it had even been advertised on national television. Dad had received a few free tickets to pass on to family or friends, and Joanne and Juliet had been given new dresses by their parents for the occasion. Even Jeremy—who tagged along because he was part of the family—had been measured for a new suit. After several days, the tailor presented him with a perfectly fitted pair of navy blue trousers, blue blazer, a white silk shirt and a floppy blue bow tie. Jeremy was quite pleased with the outfit, except for the bow tie, which he thought rather silly; but since his mother insisted that he wore it—so he did! His mother had bought a beautiful blue silk dress and dad's suit matched Jeremy's exactly, even down to the floppy bow tie.

When the day finally came, Jeremy felt embarrassed. "Look at me!" he said. "I'm all dressed up and I've got nothing to do." "Don't worry, Jeremy," said mum, "You can be in charge of the music." She handed him dad's old leather case. "I am trusting you with the most important item in the entire performance. We can't manage without music! Make sure you have it ready on stage on time." On arriving at the concert, mum, dad, Joanne and Juliet went around the back to the stage door, whereas Jeremy insisted on going through one of the front entrances. He explained to his dad that since he wasn't a performer he didn't want to use a performer's privileges.

His dad knew that what Jeremy really wanted was to have a good look around the famous building before too many people arrived. So he smiled at him and said, "Once you've had a little look around, get straight down to your seat at the front of the arena—here's one of the free tickets, I kept it for you—and you can hand the music up to me when I come on stage."

Jeremy waited until the family had gone in through the stage door and then strolled around to one of the front entrances overlooking Hyde Park. But he was perplexed to find that the doors had not yet been opened, and that there was large queue of people in front of him. Some of the ladies in the queue smiled at him, a lone little boy in a smart blue suit. "He's so cute," said one, and Jeremy blushed.

As soon as the door opened, Jeremy decided to make a dash for it, pushing through the queue. He wanted to be the first go up in the lift so that he could see the whole auditorium from the Circle; then peek into the second and grand tier boxes before finally finding his own seat in time to give dad the music. Jeremy was still trying to look important, although he looked more like a hooligan as he raced through door eight to the nearest lift and pressed the button. When the door opened, he stepped quickly inside and selected level three. Unfortunately, as he did so, his bow tie came undone and fell onto the floor outside the lift. Jeremy put the music case down on the floor of the lift, and stepped out to pick up his tie; but as he did so the lift doors closed and the lift, with the case still in it, set off for level three without him.

Jeremy wasted no time; he began running up the steps, pushing through the crowds to catch the lift. Eventually, he reached the third level and saw a small boy with ginger hair standing near the lift. He was holding a music case. "Give me that case," yelled Jeremy. He grabbed the case, but the boy held on.

They struggled together, until the clasp on the case gave way; and out fell some music—but it wasn't Jeremy's dad's music—it was music for the Trinity Boys Choir, of which the young boy was clearly a member. "Now look what you've done!" cried the boy; but, Jeremy wasn't looking! He lunged at the lift door, only then realising that the lift had not yet arrived; it had stopped to pick up people from other levels. Jeremy waited with baited breath until the lift door finally opened. Jeremy dashed into the lift; but to his dismay, the music case was gone! Jeremy strained his eyes to focus on the people who had just left the lift, and he noticed that an elderly man was carrying a black leather music case. "That's my case," shouted Jeremy, chasing the man across the Circle. But before he could reach the man, Jeremy saw him go into the North Circle Bar, open the case and take out a wallet to pay for his drink. Jeremy could see that there was nothing else inside the case, and this left him feeling somewhat bewildered. The man noticed Jeremy staring at him. "I expect you wonder why I carry an empty music case," he said. "When I come to a concert like this, I try to look as if I'm part of the action!" and he laughed.

Jeremy returned to the lift and stepped inside. There was only one thing he could do. He closed his eyes and said, "Please, God, help me!" He pressed the button and returned to the ground floor.

When the doors opened there—waiting outside the lift—was Jeremy's dad holding the music case. Jeremy didn't know what to say. His dad explained, "I was coming to find you, but when the lift opened I saw the music case on the floor and no sign of you. So I waited here until you showed up. What happened, and where's your bow tie?"

Jeremy explained what had happened and his dad laughed. "I don't think you are a bow tie person, Jeremy." he said. "But I think there's a verse in the Bible which you ought to remember: 'hold on tight to what is good'!"

The concert was excellent, and at the end of the Johnsons' performance, as all the people cheered, Mr Johnson held up his hand for silence. "There is another person who should be here on stage with us," he announced. "We couldn't perform without our music, and, so, please give a round of applause for our son Jeremy, who is responsible for making sure we have the right music for each performance." He beckoned Jeremy to join them on the stage. "But I nearly got it wrong!" said Jeremy. His dad said, "Well, together we got it right!" The audience clapped and cheered. Jeremy waved to them and felt like a star. "Thank you, God!" he said.

Biscuits in the Bus

Not being very musical himself, Jeremy did not always accompany the rest of the family to rehearsals, since he had a lot of school work to catch up on. But he always went to the concerts, which were usually in the evening, because his parents did not want to leave him in the bus by himself at night. During the day, however, as Juliet and Joanne practised their pieces he was kept well occupied with his lessons. Because Mrs Johnson was home schooling her family, it was important that he kept up to the standard she expected.

One afternoon he was working at English Comprehension. "Always read the instructions first," his mother told him. "Then carefully follow the instructions." Jeremy started his work. He was quite interested in this particular lesson, some poem or other about a dragon. Juliet and Joanne were at a concert rehearsal in the local village and mum had to just pop out and pick them up. Dad had gone to town on business, and so Jeremy would be left in charge of the bus for an hour. His mum left a mobile phone with him, in case he needed to get in touch with her before she came back.

Now, when you are working hard, you can easily work up an appetite. Earlier that week, Jeremy's mum had baked some delicious biscuits which she stored in a large porcelain jar patterned with painted daisies. Jeremy fetched the jar and decided to pace himself to eat one biscuit for each page of writing. However, this resolution was rather difficult to keep, the biscuits being so delicious; and since Jeremy was so engrossed in his work, he had only got as far as page five before his grasping fingers hit the bottom of the jar—he had eaten all of the biscuits! Just then, the phone rang; it was mum. "Jeremy," she said, "some friends of ours from one of the villages have turned up to the rehearsal. I've invited them back tor coffee. Please could you get the tray out ready for me with cups, and you'll find plenty of biscuits in the daisy jar. We'll be back in about an hour."

She rang off. Jeremy glanced at the empty jar. Well, there weren't any biscuits in there now! What could he do? Jeremy was learning, by experience, how to cope when he was in a fix; so he prayed, "Please God, I need some help here! It's over to you!" he said. He sat looking thoughtfully at the empty jar for a moment, and then remembered his mum's advice, "Always read the instructions." That gave him an idea.

He fetched her cookery book from its place on the kitchen shelf and turned to the section headed "biscuits". He gathered the ingredients from the cupboard, switched on the oven, washed his hands and put on his mother's apron. Then he carefully read the instructions, following them carefully just as he had seen his mum doing, until he had succeeded in making a batch of beautiful biscuits. When the biscuits were golden brown, like the recipe said, he carefully took them out of the oven and put them on a rack to cool; he cleared up the kitchen, laid up a tray for coffee, and then arranged the biscuits on a pretty plate. Jeremy had just finished getting everything in order, when two cars pulled up: one was his mum's and the other belonged to their guests for that afternoon.

Juliet sniffed as she entered the kitchen. "What's that smell?" she asked, suspiciously. "It's the smell of good food in a kitchen," said mum, as she prepared the coffee and began to serve her guests. The biscuits were a great success; not a crumb was left. The visitors talked for some time—apparently, one of them had gone to school with Jeremy's mum—but when they had eventually gone Jeremy volunteered to wash up.

21

When he had finished, Juliet and Joanne had gone out, and Jeremy was alone with his mum. "There is just one thing puzzling me, Jeremy," she said. "The other day I made orange flavoured cookies, but you served out ginger biscuits." Jeremy looked confused." I followed the recipe in the cookery book," he said, "they couldn't have changed in the oven!" His mum lifted the cookery book from the shelf. "Which recipe?" she asked. "There are lots of different biscuit recipes to choose from." Then she smiled. "Jeremy—are you telling me that you baked those delicious biscuits yourself? Well done! I think you've found you have got a talent after all. From now on we can call you Super Chef!"

Jeremy was pleased that at last he had a skill that was recognised. The girls were very impressed too, when they found out and so was Jeremy's dad. That night, as they all sat around in the lounge area of the bus, Jeremy announced, "You know, school work takes the energy out of me," said Jeremy, "so I keep it topped up with biscuits," and everyone laughed as he took the last ginger biscuit out of the jar.

The Village Fete

Towards the end of the summer, the Jubilant Johnsons were booked to perform at the Western County Fair. There was a huge marquee in the centre of the show ground, and they had been invited to present a concert each afternoon and evening. The show lasted for three days and on the final evening, as part of their concert, they had been asked to present a number of prizes people who had entered the various competitions during the fair.

When the official Western County Fair programmes arrived by post several weeks before the event, Jeremy read them carefully. There were competitions for the best flower arrangement, for the most succulent sausages, and even for the largest vegetable marrow. There were prizes for painting, writing, poetry, and model-making—and then, on the last page, he read about a cake making competition. This was organized by the Women's Institute, and the prize was a silver rose bowl. His mother came in at that moment and Jeremy showed her the details. His mother looked thoughtful. "Do you want to enter?" she asked. Jeremy nodded excitedly; after the success of his biscuits, he wanted to give it a try. "Then send for the entry form, and you can have a go," suggested his mum.

The entry form included a recipe for fruit cake which each competitor was to follow. Jeremy looked at the list of ingredients and realized that this was going to be an expensive enterprise. "I'm not surprised they give a silver bowl to the winner," he said. "It's a five pound entrance fee and then there's a silver bowls worth of ingredients going into the cake!" Now Jeremy was determined to make this competition all his own work, so he wasn't going to ask his mum or dad for the money, even though they had plenty. He wanted to enter himself, and so he was going to pay for himself. He looked in his savings tin, "Not much here," he thought, "£4.50. I'll need to find a way of earning some extra money."

Jeremy talked it over with his dad. "For a start, I'll pay you five pounds to hose down the bus for me," said dad. "And I'll pay you two pounds more if you clean all the windows," said his mum. Juliet said nothing; the truth was she really wished she could bake a cake, and was a bit envious of Jeremy. Joanne had earned some money of her own by playing the piano for some pensioners at a tea dance, and she offered Jeremy three pounds if he would clean her shoes.

So Jeremy filled in the entrance form, and arranged for his dad to include a cheque for five pounds and post it. When he had done all his jobs, he set off to the supermarket to buy all the ingredients for the cake: flour, butter, sugar, eggs, sultanas, raisins, glace cherries, candied peel and mixed spice. He knew he didn't need a cake tin, he had seen his mother use one for baking on the bus.

The recipe said he had to line the cake tin with greaseproof paper—he couldn't remember seeing any of that on the bus, so he bought a roll. Having paid for all his goods, Jeremy had barely two pence left, which he placed in a box on the counter, marked "Help the Aged."

When he got home, he looked at the recipe again. He read it through very carefully. He noted that the cake needed to bake slowly, for at least three hours.

He asked his mum if he could stay away from the evening performance in order to bake the cake. The bus was parked inside the showground and linked up to mains electric; and it would be light until almost 10 o'clock, so his mother agreed.

The Jubilant Johnsons set off for their afternoon performance and Jeremy set out his cake-making ingredients. First he set the oven to the correct temperature. Then he rinsed the glace cherries under the cold water tap, to remove all the syrup. He mixed the cherries, sultanas, raisins and candied peel in a big bowl. The recipe required five tablespoons of brandy, which his mother had already measured for him, and he poured this onto the fruit. He fetched another mixing bowl from the kitchen cupboard; beating the butter and sugar until it looked like cream and then beating in the eggs, one at a time.

Next he put the flour and mixed spice into a sieve and shook half of it into the creamy mix. Then he added the fruit mix and the rest of the flour. He had already lined the cake tin with two layers of grease proof paper, and so now he spooned the cake mix into the tin and put the tin into the oven. It was five o'clock; so the cake should be ready by eight o'clock. Jeremy felt very satisfied with himself; he tidied the kitchen and made himself a triple decker ham sandwich and drank two cans of coke. The oven had a glass door and Jeremy sat and watched the cake turn a lovely brown. Then at eight o'clock he took the tin out of the oven and checked that it was ready by sticking a long thin skewer into the middle. By the sight and smell of it, he was sure that this was a prize winning cake!

Jeremy waited for an hour to allow the cake to cool and carefully turned it out of the tin and put it on a wire rack to finish cooling on the window sill. He looked across to the marquee. The evening concert had just finished and people were beginning to leave. The lady who was in charge of the box office waved to Jeremy as she came towards the car park. She carried a leather bag, held tightly against her side and Jeremy guessed it held a lot of money.

Suddenly, a hooded man sprang from behind the bus and pushed the lady violently. As she fell to the ground he snatched the money bag and began to run. Jeremy yelled, "Stop, thief!", and then, as the man ran towards him—looking at him menacingly—Jeremy picked up the fruit cake and threw it at the man, hitting him right in the face. Cake crumbs scattered into the air, the man dropped the bag, trying to clear away the mess from his eyes and his nose.

People came running, and a policeman who was on duty near the entrance to the show ground grabbed the man by both arms. Someone else helped the box office lady to her feet; she was unhurt. By now a crowd had gathered and as the robber was being led away, somehow word got out that Jeremy was the hero of the day, and they gave him three rousing cheers.

Then a second crowd began to gather: a large flock of birds came spiralling down from the sky to feast on the delicious cake crumbs. With a sigh, Jeremy fetched a dust pan and brush and went out to clear up the debris.

The family was very kind to him. His dad offered to go straight to the supermarket to buy ingredients for another fruit cake.

Jeremy knew that there wasn't enough time to bake another one before the competition; the cakes had to be entered early the next morning. Juliet burst into tears when she heard what had happened and how Jeremy might have been hurt. She also felt really guilty because she hadn't given Jeremy anything towards buying the ingredients for the first cake. Joanne was crying as well, saying that she was proud to have such a brave and clever brother. Mr Johnson chose a special verse for family prayers that night. He and his wife were very relieved that Jeremy was safe. He read, *"All things work together for good to those who love God.* I think God was looking after you today, Jeremy!" "Me too, dad," said Jeremy, and everyone gave thanks to God.

The next morning, they all went up to the marquee, where the prizes were being displayed. There were silver cups, trays, medals in velvet cases and each prize had a label beside it, saying what it was for. Jeremy looked wistfully at the silver rose bowl with its label, "Best fruit cake". Then he saw another prize that caught his eye.

It was a silver knight, riding a smart silver horse. The knight carried a flag, which looked as if it was waving in the breeze although it was also made out of metal. The label beside this knight in shining armour read, "A prize for outstanding service to the community."

Jeremy gazed at the knight. He wished he knew what sort of outstanding service to the community he could do to win such a special prize. That evening's concert was another sell-out, and the lady who worked in the box office found that an extra policeman had been drafted in to stand guard over the money.

The Jubilant Johnsons performed several encores, and it was quite late when the prize giving commenced. The silver cup for the best fruit cake in the show went to a lady called Mrs Peacock. "The judges were unanimous," said the man in charge of the prizes. "Congratulations on a splendid cake." Juliet nudged Jeremy. "I think yours was better!" she said.

At last there was just the special prize to be presented. Jeremy looked at it longingly. He imagined how proudly the knight would stand in the display case back home with all the other Jubilant Johnson awards. Then to his surprise he heard his own name being called: the special prize was being awarded to him. He climbed onto the stage and all the audience clapped and cheered. The announcer allowed them to continue for a few minutes and then raised his hand for silence. "This brave boy did not hesitate to stop a dangerous thief," he said. "The thief might have been armed, but Jeremy did not hesitate. He used the only weapon that he had—a fruit cake— to stop the thief and prevent the loss of more than £2000 in takings. We have great pleasure in awarding him the special prize for outstanding service to the community." Then he handed the silver knight to Jeremy.

Jeremy's dad jumped onto the platform beside him and began to sing, in his rich tenor voice, "For he's a jolly good fellow," and every one joined in. They began to clap as Jeremy had his photograph taken with the box office lady; who said she was proud to be in the company of a "super chef" like Jeremy, who could bake burglar-stopping cakes; and everyone laughed!

Helping the Homeless

Once again the Jubilant Johnsons had been invited to give a concert for charity. Their concerts were almost always sell-out events and so the charity could be sure to raise much needed funds in this way. On this occasion they were to perform on behalf of a charity called, "Help the Homeless".

When some information about the charity arrived from its charity headquarters, Jeremy saw photographs of people sleeping in shop doorways, under cardboard boxes, and with newspapers for blankets. Jeremy couldn't imagine what it was like to be without a home. He read about people who scavenged for food through dustbins outside restaurants; eating food which other had thrown away. Then he read about others who used drugs and who were sick, living on the streets without help, and often turning to crime to support themselves. This information was a real eye-opener for Jeremy; he never knew that such a section of society existed. He became very concerned and made sure that the plight of homeless people was prayed for in family prayers.

He was also extra helpful in the weeks leading up to the concert, so that the rest of the family had plenty of time to practice and prepare.

When the night of the concert finally came, Jeremy had offered to be on duty in the entrance hall, helping to sell the programmes and signed photographs of his famous mum and dad. People were eager to buy these because it was all for a good cause. Jeremy was also secretly relieved that he hadn't been entrusted with the music on this occasion.

As the concert was about to begin, the event manager locked all the money they had taken in a safe in his office before locking the office door. A single doorman was to remain on duty throughout the performance and Jeremy decided it would be fun to stay with him and watch the people who were coming and going and walking past the theatre.

Unfortunately, it turned out that this doorman was not particularly reliable in his job. "I'm just nipping off for a cup of tea. Keep your eyes open in case the boss comes back and I'll fetch you a can of coke, right?" "Sure!" said Jeremy. Actually, he felt quite important to be in charge of the entire theatre for a few minutes. The doorman went out and closed the door behind him; and then a few minutes later it opened again. This time it wasn't the doorman. Jeremy saw a man in the door way that looked exactly like the photographs in the charity hand-outs. He was ragged, smelly and he needed a shave. As he came nearer, Jeremy noticed that he was swaying slightly and holding a green bottle in his hand. He raised the bottle to his lips, took a swig out of it and hiccupped loudly. Then he spoke, "Is this the place where they are collecting for the homeless? I'm homeless and I've come for my share."

To Jeremy's dismay, the drunken man headed for the door which led into the stalls. Jeremy ran ahead of him, and stood against the entrance. "You can't go in!" he said. "They've already started the concert." "Don't worry," said the man, "I can join in" and he started to sing, in a very loud and out of tune voice. "Roll out the barrel!" he cried, which wasn't exactly a song on the concert programme at all. Jeremy had no idea what to do. "Oh, God, help me!" he cried. The man stopped singing and looked at Jeremy angrily. "Look at me!" he said. "Look at me! I asked God to help me and I haven't heard any answer. I've got a son, somewhere in this city, if I only knew where."

"If I could find him," said Jeremy, "Perhaps he could help you. You could get your life all straightened out again." "Find him, why you'll never find…" The man's voice trailed off, for at that moment the doorman had returned. He saw Jeremy trying to stop the beggar from getting into the concert hall. Racing over to them, he grabbed the man roughly by the shoulders and turned him around. Then suddenly he stopped, unable to utter a sound. Then eventually, he managed a hoarse whisper, "Dad?' Is it you —after all these years?" He flung his arms around the old ragged man, and much to Jeremy's embarrassment, both men began to cry.

Jeremy decided he was in the way. He knew that the old man's prayer was actually being answered in front of his eyes; and that this was a private and precious moment for father and son. So he quietly opened the door to the stalls and went inside to watch the concert. Two hours later, when it was over, he was the first to leave; after all, he wanted to look like he was still officially on duty. The doorman was there, smiling. Stood next to him was someone whom Jeremy scarcely recognized. Could it be? Yes, it was! The old man—the doorman's father—had been treated to a quick shower and shave in his son's nearby flat. He was wearing a clean shirt and a tidy jacket and he was smiling more broadly than anyone else at the concert that night. He waved to Jeremy and then he pointed up to the ceiling. "There you are!" he said "God did answer my prayer!" There was no time to talk anymore, because the audience came out like a river, whirling Jeremy and the others out of their way.

Many of them wanted to buy souvenirs, and when at last, the place was quiet; a night watchman had come to take the place of the doorman. Jeremy never saw him or his father again.

When Jeremy told his family all about it, his dad said, "You were in the right place at the right time, son. Chances are the old man would never have had the courage to come in if the door man had been on duty"

His mum said, "I'm grateful God heard and answers prayer. He always does, Jeremy, if you trust him." "I'm so proud to have you as my brother," shouted Joanne; and Juliet said, "Of all the Jubilant Johnsons, you are the best! Jubilant Jeremy Johnson!" Everyone laughed, and Jeremy whispered quietly in his heart, "Thank you, God."

www.ingramcontent.com/pod-product-compliance
Lightning Source LLC
Chambersburg PA
CBHW071355130626
46556CB00005B/2190